Yours to Keep

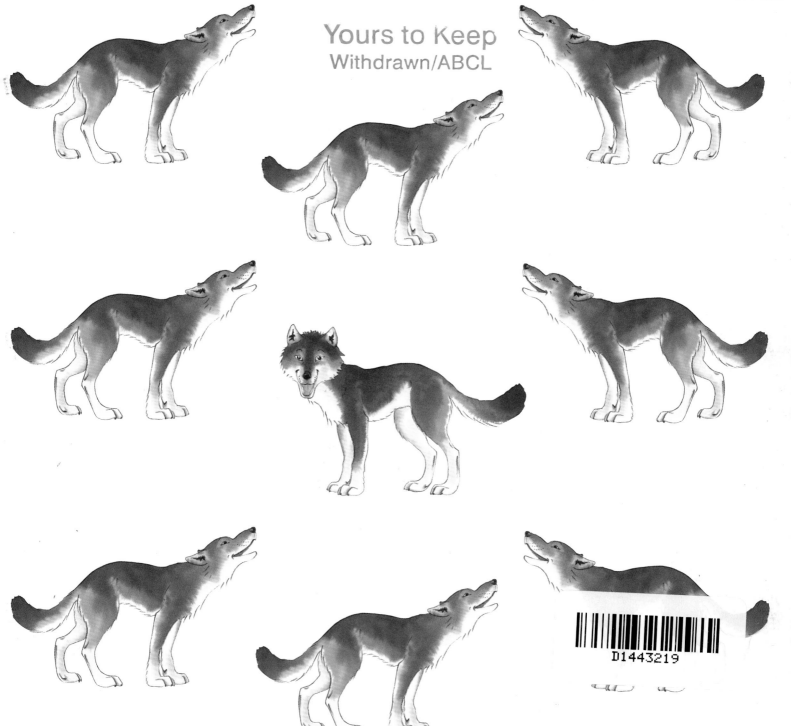

Editor: Nicole Lanctot
Production manager: Louise Kurtz
Designer: Ada Rodriguez

First published in the United States of America in 2015 by Abbeville Press,
137 Varick Street, New York, NY 10013

First published in Belgium in 2015 by Editions Mijade,
18, rue de l'ouvrage, 5000 Namur

First edition
10 9 8 7 6 5 4 3 2 1

ISBN 978-0-7892-1245-0
Library of Congress Cataloging-in-Publication Data available upon request

For bulk and premium sales and for text adoption procedures, write to Customer
Service Manager, Abbeville Press, 137 Varick Street, New York, NY 10013,
or call 1-800-ARTBOOK.

Visit Abbeville Press online at www.abbeville.com.

Wally the Wolf

Sylviane Gangloff

Abbeville Kids
A DIVISION OF ABBEVILLE PRESS
New York · London

Hello! My name is Wally,
and I am a wolf!

I am starving!

There is nothing to eat around here…

What's that you're holding?
Can I eat it?

You want me to wait? But I'm hungry!

What's he doing now?

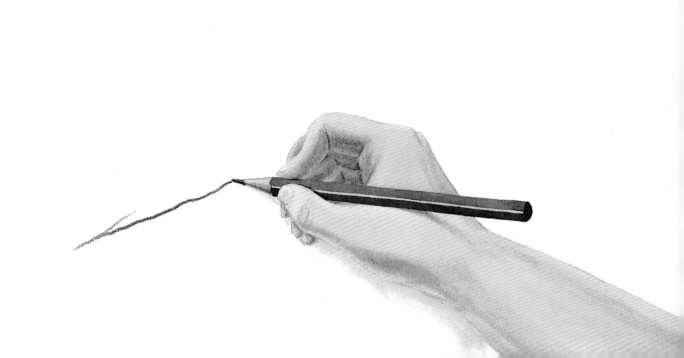

Yuck!
Wolves don't eat that!

No, thanks!
Can you please make something else?

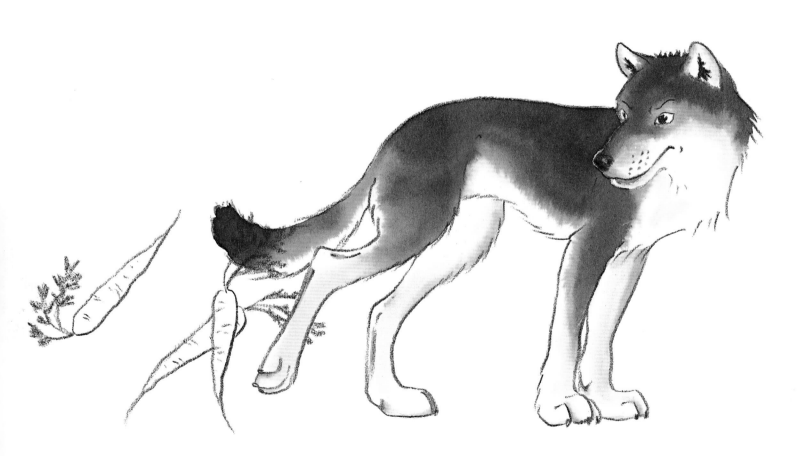

Hurry up,
I'm hungry!

What!?
He's making fun of me!

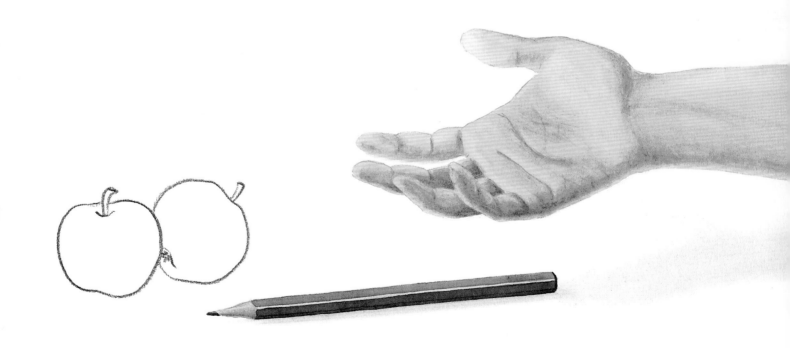

Grrr…
What if I just eat you?

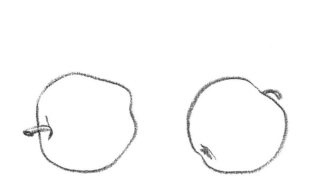

Okay, you have one last chance.

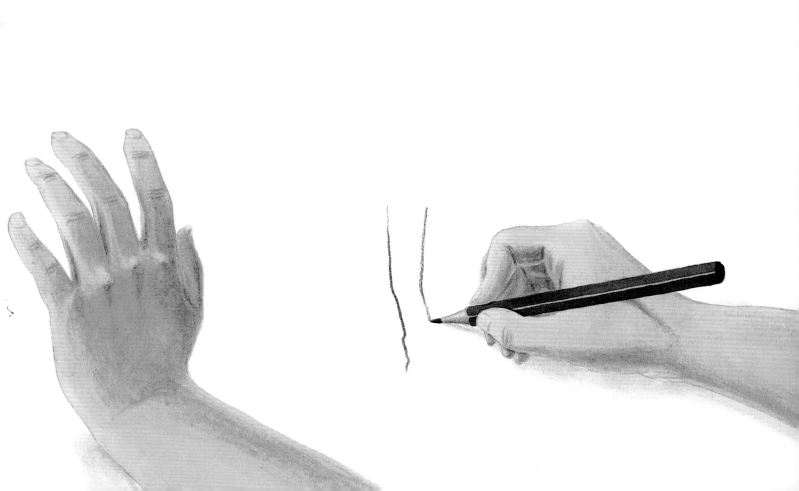

Mmm!
Now, that's better!

Something smells good!
What's in your basket?
I'd like a bite of
that cake...please?

Yum. I love cake!

That was really good. Thank you!

I get grumpy when I'm hungry…
Sorry about that. Good-bye!

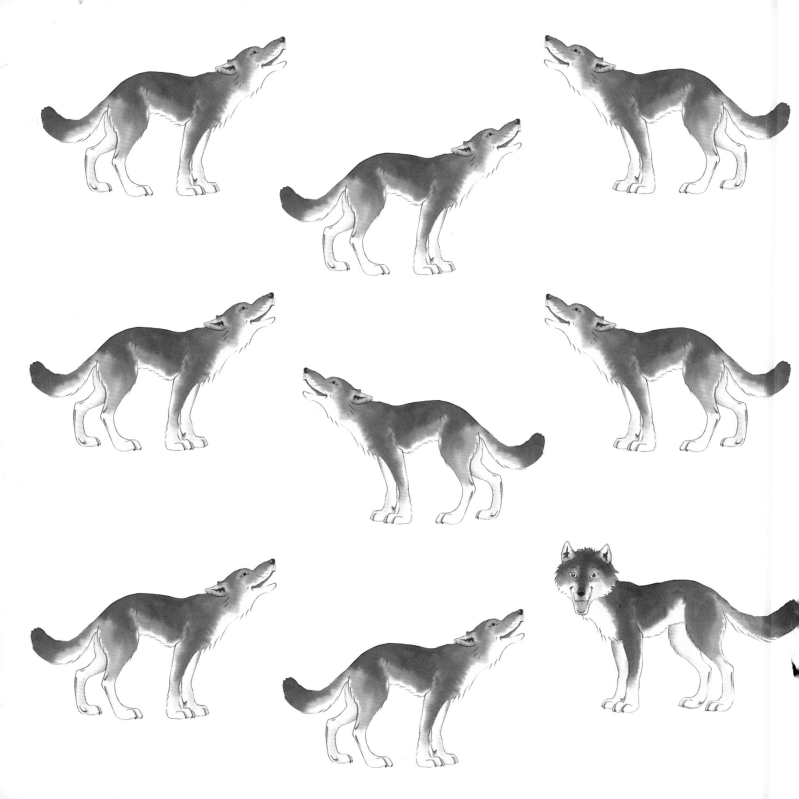